The Bears'
PICNIC

by Stan and Jan Berenstain

7 9 10 8 6

ISBN-13: 978-0-00-724259-7

© 1966 by Janice Berenstain.
A Beginner Book published by arrangement with Random House Inc., New York, USA
First published in Great Britain in 1973.
This edition published in Great Britain in 2008 by HarperCollins Children's Books.

HarperCollins Children's Books is a division of
HarperCollins Publishers Ltd, 77-85 Fulham Palace Road,
Hammersmith, London W6 8JB.

The HarperCollins website address is:
www.harpercollins.co.uk

Printed and bound in Hong Kong

Mother Bear,

put your apron away.
We are going to go
on a picnic today!

Where are we going
on our picnic, Dad?

4

To the very best place
in the world, my lad!

Now you remember
this spot, my dear.
When we were young,
we picnicked here.

Papa, I do not
like to complain,
but your wonderful spot
is next to a train!

Where are we going
now, Papa Bear?
Is there another
wonderful spot somewhere?

Don't pester me
with questions, please.
There's a place I know
right in those trees.

It is everything
a picnic spot should be.
And no one remembers
it is here but me.

What a spot! What a spot!
So quiet! So cool!
Just as it was
when I was in school.

We had a school picnic
and I won first place
for eating the most pie
in a pie-eating race.

Pop, this spot may
be very fine,
but look what it says
on that big sign!

Dad,
can you find us
another spot?
Are we having
a picnic
today, or not?

18

Now stop asking questions!
Be quiet! Stop stewing!
Your father knows
what he is doing.

To pick a spot that is
just the right one,
you have to be very
choosy, my son.

Nothing can bother
our picnic here!
Lay out the picnic
things, my dear.

24

I do not like
to say so, Dad,
but another good spot
has just gone bad.

25

I hope there's another
good spot you know.
But how much farther
do we have to go?

Why don't you use
your eyes, Small Bear?
There's a perfect place
right over there!

The grass is green.

The air is sweet.

Lay out the lunch,

and take a seat.

Hooray!

At last

we're going to eat!

Well . . .

this place is good.

I wasn't wrong.

But I know one better.

Let's move along.

33

Now take this perfect
piece of ground.
No one but us
for miles around!

Pop, you picked
the best spot yet.
But how can we picnic
with that jet?

I am very
hungry, Pop!
When is this spot-picking
going to stop?

I am getting tired.

My feet hurt, too.

Any old spot here

ought to do.

Please, Pop, please,
can't we picnic soon?
It's long past lunch.
It's afternoon!

You have to be choosy,
Pop, I know.
But what's better up here
than down below?

What's up here? . . .
I'll tell you what.
The world's most perfect
picnic spot!

As you can see,
it is perfectly clear
that *nothing* can bother
our picnic here.

No noisy crowds!
No pesky planes!
And no mosquitoes,
trucks or trains!

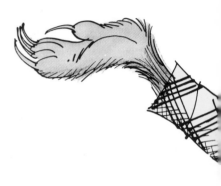

Oh-oh, Dad.

Here come the rains!

Pooh!
Rain to a bear
is nothing at all.
We'll picnic here
and let it fall.

Come back!

What kind of bears are you?

Scared of a drop

of rain or two!

Bring back that food!

This place will do.

It's dry in here.

It's warm here, too!

53

It does look warm.

Yes, I agree.

But it looks much, much
too warm for me!

Wait, now! Wait!
You wait for me!
I'll find a better spot.
You'll see.

I'll find the perfect
place to eat.
I'll find a spot
that can't be beat!
The finest spot
you've ever seen. . . .

Now,
THAT
is the kind
of place I mean!

He did it,
Mother.
Did he not?
He found the perfect
picnic spot!

Read them **together**, read them **alone**, read them **aloud** and make **reading fun!**
With over **50 wacky stories** to choose from, now it's **easier** than **ever** to find the
right **Dr. Seuss** books for your child – just let the **back cover colour** guide you!

Here's a great selection to choose from:

Blue back books
for sharing with your child

Dr. Seuss's ABC
A Fly Went By
The Bears' Picnic
The Bike Lesson
The Eye Book
The Foot Book
Go, Dog, Go!
Hop on Pop
I'll Teach My Dog 100 Words
Inside Outside Upside Down
Mr. Brown Can Moo! Can You?
One Fish, Two Fish, Red Fish, Blue Fish
The Shape of Me and Other Stuff
There's a Wocket in my Pocket!

Green back books
for children just beginning to read on their own

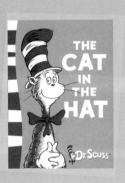

A Fish Out of Water
And to Think That I Saw It on Mulberry Street
Are You My Mother?
The Bears' Holiday
Bears On Wheels
The Best Nest
The Cat in the Hat
The Cat in the Hat Comes Back
Come Over To My House
The Digging-est Dog
Fox in Socks
Gerald McBoing Boing
Green Eggs and Ham
Happy Birthday to YOU
Hunches in Bunches
I Can Read With My Eyes Shut!
I Wish That I Had Duck Feet
Marvin K. Mooney Will You Please Go Now!
Oh, Say Can You Say?
Oh, the Thinks You Can Think!
Ten Apples Up on Top
Wacky Wednesday

Yellow back books
for fluent readers to enjoy

The 500 Hats of Bartholomew Cubbins
Daisy-Head Mayzie
Did I Ever Tell You How Lucky You Are?
Dr. Seuss's Sleep Book
Horton Hatches the Egg
Horton Hears a Who!
How the Grinch Stole Christmas!
If I Ran the Circus
If I Ran the Zoo
I Had Trouble in Getting to Solla Sollew
The Lorax
McElligot's Pool
Oh, the Places You'll Go!
On Beyond Zebra
Scrambled Eggs Super!
The Sneetches and other stories
Thidwick the Big-Hearted Moose
Yertle the Turtle and other stories